SHERBET AND SHENANIGANS

A BELLE HARBOR COZY MYSTERY
(BOOK 9)

SUE HOLLOWELL

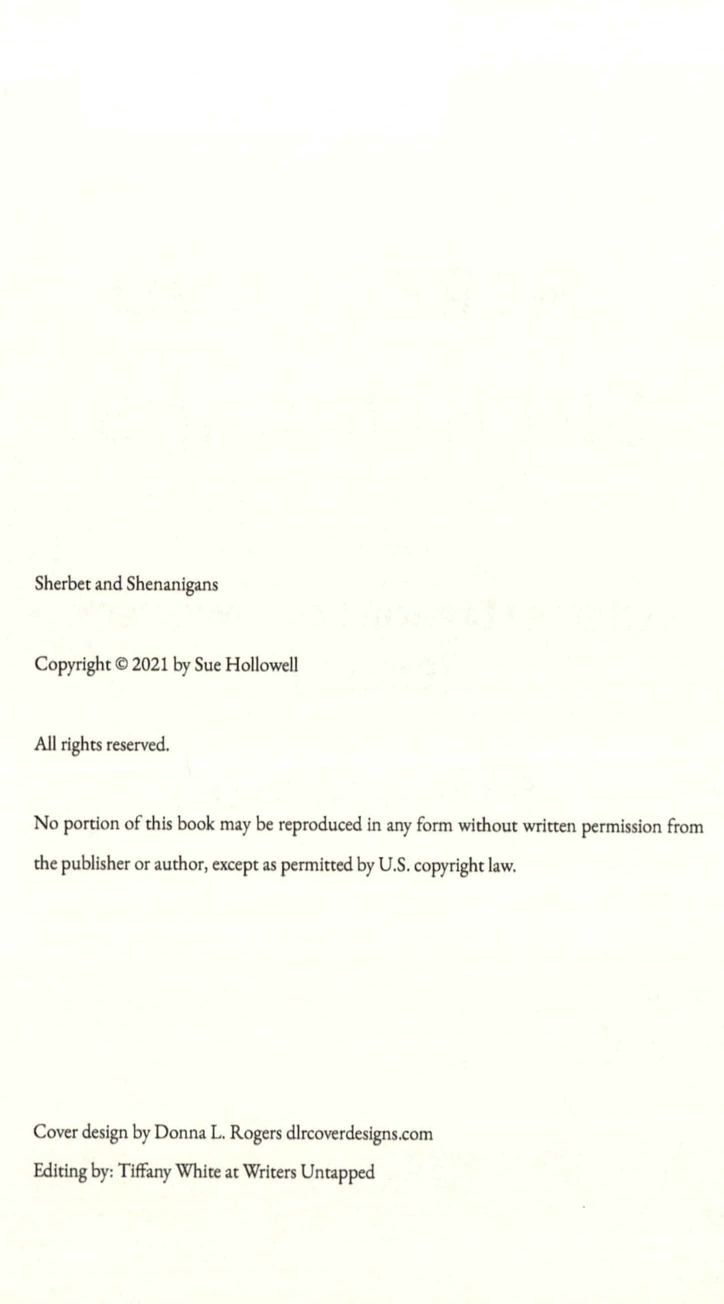

Sherbet and Shenanigans

Cover design by Donna L. Rogers dlrcoverdesigns.com
Editing by: Tiffany White at Writers Untapped

CONTENTS

CHAPTER ONE

Folding tables covered in white tablecloths lined the outside of the room. The silent auction items donated from businesses all over Belle Harbor were organized in an orderly way, each one with a piece of paper next to it for attendees to write their bids. I strolled the room, perusing anything of interest, or not. The money would be used for a good cause, and anything I won could be gifted or donated to someone else if it wasn't something for me.

Daffy Taffy donated five pounds of various flavors of salt-water taffy. I quickly moved on from that item, reminiscing about my brother's recent visit and the handfuls of taffy we consumed during his time here. My heart clenched. Not willing to trade my new life in this town for anything, I had decided more frequent visits to my brother's traveling baseball team and my parents in Boston would make me happy. That revelation surprised, or more accurately, shocked me.

Time was a barrier to making that happen. Opening my new bakery location had consumed every waking moment, forcing me to hire part-time help to keep some sanity. My baking partner Linda's efficiency meant we could produce more than double what two people normally could do. As word of the bakery had traveled, we'd only gotten busier. The newest addition to our team was a part-timer, helping with many of the non-baking chores. Dexter had been a hoot, was an extremely hard worker, and ate his weight in baked goods every shift. I may have to give him a quota or teach him to bake his own.

Continuing to stroll the tables, I was pleased with the number of auction items donated. This charity was a passion project for Uncle Jack and had been for many years. The money raised was provided to a local farm who raised dogs as companions for single elderly people. Part of the funds were used to pay the ongoing food and veterinary bills for those adopted. I stopped and looked around at the growing crowd, milling about the silent part of the auction and bidding. The main event was scheduled to start shortly, the long-time auctioneer always pulling in record levels of donations.

Several getaways in nearby resorts tempted me to bid, and I considered a trip with Justin. He and I were getting serious, and although we had been on several adventures together, he had finally asked me out on our very first official date. It didn't feel any different from previous outings with him, and then again, my heart said otherwise. I really enjoyed our relationship and was nervous for it to change but tried to focus on how it could be even better. I didn't want to get my hopes to high. But was there a scenario where we ended up married?

Smiling big, I grabbed a pen next to the Paradise Hills Resort and wrote my name on the bid sheet. This round of items would expire soon, and it wouldn't be long before I found out if there was a trip with Justin in my future.

"I hope you'll take me if you win that." Justin sidled up to me, giving me a quick hug.

Tilting my head, I kept silent. Justin's presence calmed me, and he was so easy to be with. Was this my future husband? I shook my head, scattering my thoughts.

"No?" he asked, eyes big, stepping back, placing his hand on his chest as if I had severely wounded him with my response.

Grinning, I said, "I was thinking of something else." Linking arms with him, we strolled through the growing crowd rushing around for the last-minute bids on their favorite items.

This event brought out almost the entire town. "See anything you can't live without?" I asked Justin as we continued along the tables of silent auction items.

Lifting his arm toward the live auction items, he said, "A surfboard over there has my name on it." We migrated in the direction he pointed: an ocean-blue colored board that stood at least a foot taller than Justin.

"No way you're ever getting me on one of those things," I said. "I need something more solid surrounding me."

"Never say never." He chuckled, rubbing his hand on the smooth resin surface.

"Ladies and gentlemen," came the booming auctioneer's voice over the speakers. "You have sixty seconds for round one in the silent auction. Hurry over to get your favorite items before someone else does."

Looking at Justin, I grabbed his hand, pulling him across the room to the Paradise Hills Resort bid sheet. Dang! Someone outbid me. I looked around to see if the item was being stalked by the winning bidder. I certainly would not arm wrestle someone for it. The crowd sped around, following the auctioneer's advice as he juiced up the excitement. Picking up the pen, I wrote my name on the next blank row.

"Time's up! Pens down!" the auctioneer bellowed.

My arms prickled with goosebumps as I thought of another fun adventure for Justin and me. "Congratulations," he said, his eyes practically sparkling.

"Can I get a picture of you two with your winning item?"

I swiveled around to see Robin Sullivan of the Belle Harbor Gazette, poised with her camera in front of her face, ready to capture the moment.

Looking at Justin, I shrugged, picking up the certificate and holding it in front of me, Justin gently leaning in as Robin snapped the picture.

"Thank you," she said, letting the camera settle to her mid-section at the end of the strap, keeping it at the ready to capture other auction moments. She had done a beautiful piece on Uncle Jack and Linda's engagement, telling a lovely story of their backgrounds and how they met.

Grateful for the attention, I was convinced her articles boosted business at the bakery. "You should come by the bakery again. We've always got new things we're trying," I suggested. It never hurt to ask.

Gazing around the room, she replied, "Yeah, sure," distracted by the bustle of activity for the second round of silent auction items about to close. With a dismissive wave, she departed, speeding around the room, sticking her nose over several bid sheets.

"Why don't we take a seat?" Justin suggested, holding up his bid paddle with number twenty-seven, ready to take that surfboard home as his own.

Meeting us mid-room, Uncle Jack beamed, rubbing his hands together. "Our best turnout yet," he said. "If my calculations are correct, I'm hoping we raise enough to place another twenty dogs and continue the care for the fifty already placed." The Dogs for Seniors program had received national attention, not just for providing companions to single elderly people, but for financing the continued care of the dogs after adoption, even transportation to veterinary appointments.

Justin and I sat in metal folding chairs near the front auctioneering podium.

"I need to do one last check to make sure Clint is ready," Unkie said and disappeared from the room.

The clock on the wall had passed the deadline for bidding on items in the second round, but nobody had announced the closure. The volume of chatter from the crowd escalated as I heard sneers complaining of Clint's inability to run a fair competition.

Linda approached from our left, bending so that we could hear. "I wonder what's going on," she said, looking at the confused faces surrounding us. "I better go find Jack." She exited the main community center room.

I only hoped this blip on the radar didn't diminish enthusiasm for bidding to support this noble cause.

"Where's Clint?" someone yelled. Yes, indeed, where was Clint, and where was Unkie? Something wasn't right, and I stood to go find out what it was before the crowd came any more unglued.

A blood-curdling scream emanated from the hallway to our left, from a voice very familiar. Linda.

CHAPTER TWO

y mind raced with thoughts of Uncle Jack splayed on the ground, some sort of health condition doing him in. Justin sprung up and sprinted down the hallway, the crowd's demeanor shifting from irritation to concern. Why did my brain always go from zero to calamity in two seconds? The audience stayed in place, apparently assuming the interrupted auction might not be happening as planned. Whispers started as heads bowed together, fingers pointing as everyone tried to make sense of the situation.

Following immediately on Justin's heels, I met up with him in the room set aside for the auctioneer's preparations to see Clint face down on the brown and tan diamond-shaped linoleum floor, his light blue suede jacket marred with Uncle Jack's auction donation sticking out from the center. Someone had stabbed Clint in the back with the antique knife. Justin bent to check for a pulse on Clint's neck, gently touching him just above his jacket collar.

Shaking his head and standing, Justin said, "He's dead."

To my right, Uncle Jack had enveloped Linda in his arms as she wept into his chest, sniffling. "Who would have done this?"

Unkie patted her back, laying his head onto Linda's, closing his eyes.

Click, click came from my left side as Robin had entered completely unnoticed. Of course a dead body was news, but could you at least give it a few minutes?

Reading my mind, Justin held his arms out, taking a couple of steps toward the door. "We need to get out of here. I'm sure Barney will be right here to take over," he said, shepherding us into the hallway.

Robin stood on tiptoes, attempting to view into the room past Unkie and Linda in the entryway. She extended her arms with the camera above her head, snapping several more shots just as Barney arrived.

Pulling her arm gently down, Barney said, "Robin, not now."

She huffed and loudly snapped the lens cap onto the camera. "The press will not be denied," she proclaimed.

Barney looked around at the assembled group, focusing on Justin, who seemed to be the one holding his cool the most. "Justin." Barney gestured toward the room with Clint where they disappeared and shut the door.

Stepping toward Uncle Jack and Linda, Robin began, "Linda, what happened? What did you see?"

I couldn't take any more of this. There would be plenty of time for inquisition later when Barney did a full investigation. There weren't many people in Belle Harbor that hadn't come out to the auction, including the police chief. I suspected he was hopeful for a night of enjoyment and goodwill, working a murder the last thing on his mind.

Turning my back on Robin and moving next to Unkie and Linda, I said, "I'm so sorry." I leaned in and gave Uncle Jack a side squeeze.

Peering over Linda's head, his eyes softened and he gave me a slight lips-pursed smile.

Linda straightened up and sniffed, stepping away from Uncle Jack. "Who would want to hurt him?" Shaking her head as her short silver hair swung around her face, she continued, "He loved this auction."

Clint Harshman was a professional auctioneer, traveling the country to host charity auctions, sometimes raising millions of dollars. His time for this local Belle Harbor charity was donated for the good of the cause.

"Linda, you knew Clint, didn't you?" Robin asked, that inquisitive reporter mode always on. She was always interrogating people for a story, or at least that's what it felt like.

Linda nodded, drifting back into Uncle Jack's embrace. What was Robin getting at? Everyone knew everyone else in this town, and given Clint's minor celebrity status, how could you not?

Taking a few steps away, Uncle Jack pivoted the opposite direction from Robin, glaring at her over Linda's head. I agreed. Time and place, Robin. We all jumped as the door opened, Justin leading Barney from the room, Barney quietly closing the door behind them. Justin stepped over to me, standing so close our arms touched. I tried to read his stoic face to figure out what went on behind closed doors and why Barney would only allow Justin inside with him.

Confronting Barney, Robin uncapped her camera, poised to capture the breaking news. "Chief, the people need to know," she started, looking around for support. Reaching inside her pocket she pulled out a small, spiral notebook with a pen attached, ready to report.

Waving her off, Barney quietly asked, "Robin, have you ever known me to hold back on a story?"

Shaking her head, she demurely stepped back.

Justin's movement to interlace his fingers with mine was slight enough not to attract any attention. He squeezed and held firm as

Barney turned toward Linda and Uncle Jack. It was clear the auction would be postponed, and I expected Barney would want Unkie to take the lead in letting the attendees know. I was sure there would be disappointment, but when it did resume people would be even more generous, given the sullen circumstances from today.

"Jack," Barney started in his most official voice. I would help Unkie however he needed to wrangle the crowd and close out the auction until it could resume. Barney continued, "I'm sorry. But you are under arrest for the murder of Clint Harshman."

I stumbled backward, Justin's grip the only thing that kept me from tumbling to the floor. Looking at him and back at Barney, I croaked, "Barney." Justin reeled me into his arms, holding tight.

Unkie pinched his eyes closed, his lips on Linda's head as she sobbed. "Jack, no!" Unkie released her into Justin's grasp. Turning toward Barney, she said, "Barney, how could you? Jack is the most gentle man I've ever met."

Robin furiously wrote in her notebook, looking at each person in the area to capture all of the details.

Uncle Jack rotated with his back to Barney and reached his arms behind him to be placed in cuffs. Why was he not saying anything to defend himself?

"Unkie?" I inquired.

Was there any possibility he had done this? It was the knife he donated that was protruding from Clint's back. I replayed the sequence of events in my head just prior to hearing Linda's scream coming from the hallway. Uncle Jack had said he was checking on Clint given the live auction was about to begin. Justin and I were seated and waiting. I closed my eyes, trying to recall any other movements in the moments just before my world was rocked.

Without a word, Barney led Uncle Jack through a side door that led to the parking lot of the community center, kindly avoiding all of the inquiring minds still waiting to hear what was happening.

"This is going to be front page news tomorrow. This reporting might just finally win me a prize," Robin gleefully stated, heading back to the large room.

The hallway quieted with the three of us stunned with what had just happened. "Linda." I grabbed her arms, my wits beginning to slowly return. "He didn't do this. We will get to the bottom of it," I said with much more gusto than I felt. Oh, Unkie.

CHAPTER THREE

No matter what was happening in my life, I had an obligation to my customers. And thankfully, my baking provided a respite from the confusing events of yesterday. I still wasn't sure when I woke up whether it was a horrible nightmare or that my uncle had actually been hauled off to jail for the murder of the auctioneer. Pinching my eyes closed, I desperately tried to envision a new clue that could provide an answer to free Unkie. No way could I let my mind go the place where there was even the remotest possibility that he had done this.

Everyone had their breaking point, but nothing in Uncle Jack's makeup would even come close to resembling a person capable of murder. I knew that from the deepest depths of my gut. His disposition was that of a man who kept a balanced perspective, even amid the worst of circumstances. It wasn't as if he was under a lot of stress, given his and Linda's recent engagement, and his business was booming. No major life stresses that I knew of that could prompt a person to snap, much less take the life of another human being.

Linda and I had silently gone about our baking preparations for the day, finishing our work in record time. With our display cases bursting with the latest new confection brainchild from Linda, tropical cupcakes, we set about cleaning the kitchen. The samples with almond filling, topped with coconut frosting, had flown off the shelves. The baking therapy, along with doing the dishes, provided a comforting routine in the depths of anguish for Uncle Jack's circumstances.

Barney had texted me earlier that we wouldn't be able to visit Unkie until tomorrow. That felt eons away for me and probably even longer for Linda. My brain swirled with thoughts about how we could spring him from the joint. The only answer was that another viable suspect must be found. My mission was never clearer. Given Clint's international travels, the contacts he made would be extensive. But someone had made their way to our little town and attended the auction to do the deed. Were they still in town or had they escaped detection and possibly gotten away with murder?

The pressure on my chest increased as I felt the sense of urgency to gather clues as fast as I could to solve this. I wouldn't let my mind go the place yet where there was a scenario that kept Uncle Jack in jail indefinitely.

"Yo," came a cracking voice as Dexter bounded through the kitchen door. Our part-time teenage employee strolled his lanky body next to Linda, giving her a side squeeze. "What can I do, boss?" he asked, heading my direction, bobbing his head toward Linda. "How is she doing?" he whispered.

I shrugged. What could I say? She was devastated and trying to keep busy to distract herself. Pointing to a stack of dirty cupcake pans, I said, "Those need to be washed. And when we are finished here, if you would make the delivery to Mocha Joe's."

Dexter saluted and headed to the sink, grabbing the sprayer to dislodge the crusty pieces from the pan. With a giant squirt, he splashed water in the sink, an errant stream heading straight for Linda's apron.

"Hey," she squealed, cracking a smile for the first time since the auction.

"So sorry, Linda. Not sure what happened," Dexter said, turning toward her, another spray emitting right at her head.

"Dexter," I said, stepping forward to rescue Linda from the shower, handing Linda a towel.

She grinned from ear-to-ear, shaking her head. "It's OK," she said, wiping her face and removing her apron to replace it with a dry one.

"Believe it or not, I needed that to get me out of my funk. It will not do Jack any good if I sit around sulking."

Dexter glanced at me, shaking his head, his tall body slumping, and said, "I really don't know what happened."

Retrieving a dozen empty delivery boxes from the shelf, I opened up the blue and white Luna's Bakery and Cafe logo containers to fill with our order for Mocha Joe's. "Why don't you finish up there and then you can take these over to Joe?" I chuckled at the antics, thoroughly pleased with my growing team. Dexter worked his tail off, had a great attitude, and was a superb kid, even if he had a teenage goof now and then.

"You got it, boss." Dexter turned and, carefully aiming the nozzle, ensured the water stayed in the sink this time, or at least in front of him as his shirt was getting soaked. That kid was going to provide us endless entertainment.

Moving over to the worktable, I pulled several trays of muffins and cupcakes toward me, filling the boxes. The sweetness of the frosting prompted my smile in memory of my grandma. Her signature cream-filled cupcakes were one of our bestsellers, and for good reason. Linda and I tried to improve on that with our own flavors, but nothing stood up to the classic.

Dexter's awkward movements clanged the pans around the sink area as he finished with the first round of dishes for the day. By the time he returned from his delivery, we would have a sink full and ready for him. With the last pan placed in the drying rack, he wheeled the delivery wagon to the side of the counter and lifted the boxes and slightly wobbled. I couldn't watch. I just had to hope for the best, busying myself with setting up the next set of ingredients for our newest experiment: biscotti.

From the corner of my eye, I saw Dexter successfully load the boxes as he wheeled the wagon out the side door, waving. "Bye, all. Be back soon," he said.

As soon as the door clicked shut, Linda and I looked at each other, bent over, holding our stomachs laughing.

"I'm not sure whether to laugh or cry," she said, approaching the worktable to my right, head bowed.

"We'll figure this out, Linda. I'm sure of it," I said, exuding more confidence than I felt. If you didn't know Uncle Jack and were an outsider observing this situation, you would have him convicted from the clues and sent to prison for decades. I shuddered and shook out my arms to rid the stress and heinous thoughts.

"Let me know what I can do," Linda muttered, fidgeting with a dishtowel. "I feel so helpless."

I stopped pouring ingredients into the mixer and stood in front of Linda, grabbing each of her hands, looking deeply into her eyes. "I've got some ideas I'm going to run by Fiona. Why don't you join us tomorrow and we'll all put our heads together?"

Linda sniffled, tipping her tear-streaked face to the left. I had to be strong for her and Unkie, hoping Fiona would have some ideas. My proximity to the situation was keeping me from seeing the obvious. The murderer was at the auction. We just needed to ceremoniously proceed with a process of elimination. I squeezed Linda's hands as she departed the kitchen to the lobby, our first customers of the day arriving.

CHAPTER FOUR

If only the pace of customers today sufficed to keep Linda completely distracted. Maybe we could talk about a possible remodel I had in mind. The bakery had only been open a short time in this new location, but people weren't too keen on staying inside long after they got their treats. I was confident that outdoor seating would be more useful and was looking forward to Fiona's experience in expanding her bar the same way.

"Hello, my dear," I heard Linda say, along with a third voice.

I poured the remaining ingredients into the mixer so I didn't lose my place, then wiped my hands on my apron and headed to the lobby to make sure she wasn't overwhelmed with early bird customers.

Entering the brightly lit room, I spotted only three people, Linda, her niece Jenna, and Robin the newspaper reporter, standing in the center of the room.

"Hello ladies," I greeted, lifting my hand in a wave. Although we were technically closed for another half hour, we typically unlocked the door early, just in case a few people needed their pastries before sunrise. The light outside bathed the gentle morning waves in a soft pink shade, the white foam looking like a yummy frosting color we needed to make.

Both Jenna and Robin greeted me, while Linda and her niece huddled together. Approaching me, Robin looked back at Linda before she said, "I'd like to do a story on Jack."

Whipping their heads toward us in unison, Linda and Jenna simultaneously said, "What?!" Linda's face was drawn at the mention of her beloved fiancé.

What in the world was Robin's angle? Sure, she was the lead reporter for the paper, and a murder was certainly front-page news in Belle Harbor, but I sincerely expected before long that Unkie would be free and clear, another suspect going away for the crime.

"Sorry to be the messenger, but this story is hot right now," Robin said, glancing back at Linda. "I'm just doing my job." She held out both hands, palms up with a notebook in one of them, attempting a conciliatory pose. Pivoting toward Linda, she continued, "It would help if I could interview you for some background too."

Linda's hand flew to her mouth as she shook her head, sniffing.

Rescuing her, I said, "Maybe another time. Plus, Uncle Jack is innocent. He'll be released anytime. I think your time would be better spent finding the actual killer."

"Do you know something I don't?" Robin asked, notebook and pen poised to jot down any relevant details.

"Only that Jack has a heart of gold and could never do something like that," I firmly replied, sauntering toward the door, trying to get Robin to follow me and exit. The longer Unkie stayed in jail, the more Robin would pester us for a story. Yes, she was only doing her job, but she seemed to be enjoying the fact that Uncle Jack had been arrested.

"How about just a few background questions for now?" She poised her pen. "The murder weapon was an antique knife that Jack had donated to the auction, correct?"

Jenna guided Linda to a nearby table to sit as it became obvious Robin wasn't leaving without something.

"Yes," I curtly replied.

Robin pounded her notebook, writing. "And do you know the origin of it?"

I moved to the door and opened it, holding it for Robin's departure. "If we think of anything else, we'll let you know."

Accepting the hint that she wasn't getting anything else for now, Robin slid past me and left. I closed the door and locked it so we could recover from that disruption until time to open. Jenna continued comforting Linda as the room felt like the air had been sucked out of it.

"I'm sorry, Aunt Linda. I didn't know what she wanted when she came in," Jenna said, gently patting Linda's back.

"It's OK. I know there are lots of questions. And everyone wants to find the murderer," she stuttered. "Nobody more than me." Standing, Linda pressed down her apron, looking around and wiping her tears with the back of her hand. "And we've got a bakery to run. So let's get to it."

"Jenna?" I asked, unaware of the purpose of her visit.

Shaking her head, she said, "Oh, yeah," and looked toward Linda. "I wanted to see if you want to go to the farm with me to visit the dogs up for adoption."

Getting away would do wonders for distracting Linda from the traumatic events, and I was grateful for Jenna's suggestion.

Linda shrugged. "I don't want to go too far. Jack might need me," she replied. There wasn't anything she could do for him while he was in the slammer.

"You know," I quietly started, looking at Jenna, "a distraction might be just what the doctor ordered."

Linda stood silently.

Continuing, I asked, "What would Uncle Jack want you to do?"

Pinching a slight smile, Linda replied, "He would insist I go." Her smile widened as she looked at Jenna. "I would love to."

"It's just going to take some time, but he will get out," I said, wondering how I could expedite his release. Until Barney had more evidence pointing to another suspect, he couldn't let go of the one he had.

A light knock at the door reminded me it was time to open. Turning to see a line outside, I smiled. That would occupy Linda for a while.

"We've got customers to serve," Linda said, heading to the door, her shoulders back and head up. She smiled widely, opening the door to the eager crowd.

"Jenna, could I ask you a favor if you have a bit of time?" I stepped out of the way of customers hurrying to the display case to make their choices.

"Of course," she said, stepping over to my side.

"Uncle Jack has his friend Mick running the antique shop while he is out of commission," I said, hurrying behind the counter to package up purchases in to-go bags.

Linda had her game face on, serving the customers efficiently as everyone took their goodies and headed out for their day.

"OK," Jenna said.

"Would you be able to hang out here for a bit so I can go check on him?" I asked.

Jenna grinned. "Of course. Let me go wash up and grab an apron."

"Thank you so much. Just until Dexter gets back. Shouldn't be too long," I said. "And if you enjoy it, maybe you'd consider a part-time position." I grinned, only half joking.

I needed to accelerate my recruitment or Linda and I would burn out. Truthfully, the longer Uncle Jack was in jail, the more concerned I got about his antique shop. His new employee Carlos was only part time, and I might just have to split my day helping run his store. Uncle Jack and his brother Frank had started Checkered Past Antiques decades ago, and it would crush us both if he couldn't keep it going. Not only did I have to get him out of jail and off the suspect list for Clint's murder, I needed to ensure his store didn't suffer until then. How in the world was I going to pull this off?

CHAPTER FIVE

The rest of the first rush of customers exited, leaving Linda to tidy up the lobby before the next group arrived. They seemed to appear in hoards, either feast or famine.

"Will you be OK if I duck out for just a bit?" I asked.

With that initial group of customers keeping her occupied, Linda's demeanor seemed to perk up. I hoped she could stay out of her head and the downward spiraling thoughts for a while.

She smiled. "Yes. I'll be fine and Jenna will be here." Linda picked up a stray napkin, gently folding it and placing it in her pocket.

"And it shouldn't be too long before Dexter gets back too," I said, considering a bonus for that kid if he continued to entertain Linda the way he did before he left on the deliveries.

She chuckled, shaking her head, likely at the memory of her getting doused with the sink sprayer. "He's such a good kid," she said.

I removed my apron and tucked it on a shelf under the cash register and headed out the door. The sun had completely risen but was not yet warming up the temperature to what it would be in the heat of the day. The beach was sparsely populated at this early hour, most people walking with a cup of coffee in their hand from Mocha Joe's. If my timing was right, I should see Dexter on his return trip to the bakery.

Mick should have the antique shop open by now. With Carlos so new and Mick not having much experience running the place, I was doubtful the arrangement would work.

"Hey boss." Dexter raised his hand, the empty wagon trailing behind him. It looked like the delivery was a success. With him, I expected the unexpected. And Linda was right, he was a good kid.

We stopped mid-sidewalk, and I said, "I'm heading to Uncle Jack's. I'm sure Linda will have some things for you to do." I waved my arm in the direction I had just come from.

"Sure thing," he said and loped away as if he didn't have a care in the world.

Being around him kept me on my toes, but his calm manner reminded me of Justin, one of the most relaxed people I knew.

Up ahead, I saw light emanating from the window of the antique shop, a good sign that at least someone had arrived and opened up. I pushed open the door, the squeak announcing my arrival.

Carlos and Mick had their heads bowed together in the back of the store, reviewing a book. Mick raised his head.

"Hi Tilly," he said as he returned to his conversation with Carlos.

As I navigated to the back of the store, I saw a very pregnant younger woman seated at the small table Uncle Jack kept for the frequent coffee chats. Those were less frequent now that my bakery had moved from the corner of his shop to my own space. I made a note to myself to add more of them back into my routine. For now, top priority was keeping the shop running—and figuring out how to spring Unkie.

"I don't think we've met," I said, extending my arm toward the woman, who struggled to stand. "I'm Tilly, Jack's niece."

Unable to easily hoist herself out of the chair, the woman responded, "I'm Annie, Carlos's wife." After several attempts, she pushed herself up and shook my hand.

"Tilly, can you explain Jack's books to us?" Mick stepped away, hands on his skinny hips. "I'm sure there's a rhyme and a reason, but we can't figure it out. And I know we're going to get really busy." He rubbed his hands nervously together just as a customer entered the store.

Annie slowly lowered herself back into her seat, loudly exhaling. By the looks of it, she was pretty far along.

I moved to the other side of the table to see what Mick and Carlos were looking at. "I think the way he did this, and let's keep it simple for now, is just write as much information about each item you ring up. That way when he's back, if it needs to be adjusted, he'll know what it is," I said. Everything we did needed to be with the assumption Unkie would soon return to his normal life. Any other scenario was unfathomable.

The customer approached with a small vase in her hand and asked, "Is this something you could ship?"

Carlos and Mick looked at each other as I inserted myself, responding, "We'd be happy to."

The customer placed the vase on the counter. "I have a few more items I'm interested in too." Well, at least the money would continue coming in, even if we weren't all that swift at the bookkeeping.

"Oof," Annie loudly said from her chair, scooting to the edge.

"Excuse me, ma'am," came the voice of Florence, who owned the bookstore next door. This was getting to be a circus for this early in the morning. While my relationship with Florence had improved, she could definitely throw a curveball now and then. She approached our customer with another bag labeled with her store name. "You forgot your other package." Looking around, Florence asked, "What's going on?"

A legitimate question, given the disorganization of the crew attending the store with Uncle Jack's obvious absence.

"Mick volunteered to run the store until—" I stopped. We all knew until what.

A loud moan came from Annie as she attempted to stand. Carlos approached her, encouraging her to stay seated as he looked around, his eyes wide.

Annie's voice now echoed throughout the store. "Carlos!" she yelled, gripping the arm of the chair with one hand and her moving belly with the other.

Mick stepped back, watching the scene unfold as Carlos asked, "Is it time?"

Annie squeezed her eyes closed, nodded, and let out another yell, each one louder than the first.

"I'll call 9-1-1," I offered, not familiar with childbirth and the only thing I could think of doing.

"There's not time," Florence said, moving to stand right in front of Annie. "Carlos, find blankets, towels, any cloth you can." Florence pointed directly at Carlos. She knelt in front of Annie, gripping both of her hands. Without eye contact with Mick, she ordered him to help Carlos. "You're doing great," Florence cooed to Annie.

Great?! What was happening? I couldn't believe Annie was having her baby right now in the store, and of all things, that Florence had stepped up to deliver it.

Quickly turning toward the customer, Mick asked, "Sorry, can you come back later?"

Silently nodding, the woman stepped to the side, making way for the medics when they arrived. She would certainly have a story to tell later.

Mick had returned with two cushions removed from the chairs in the coffee seating area, and Carlos had somehow found a blanket to cover them. Florence eased Annie to the floor as she let out a loud yowl.

The 9-1-1 operator informed me that the medics were on their way, and he instructed me to remain on the phone until they arrived.

As if she had done this her entire life, Florence instructed Annie and had positioned Carlos to Annie's side to hold her hand. Uncle Jack would regret missing this experience. I wondered how he would have responded to a woman going into labor in his store. I expected he had seen quite a few things in the almost four decades of running a business, but I doubt a baby being delivered was one of them.

Florence's soothing voice talked Annie through each contraction as the medics entered the store to take it from here. We all stepped away to allow some privacy for the parents-to-be.

CHAPTER SIX

The drab industrial green walls of the jail lobby were what you might expect from a government organization. Linda and I entered the quiet space and proceeded to the glass enclosed office to check in for our visit with Uncle Jack. I had never been to visit anyone in jail before, and I hadn't a clue about how this was going to go. The attendant behind the window slid it open and pointed to a piece of paper on a clipboard in front of us.

"Sign in, put your valuables in a locker." She gestured to the wall on our left, lined with ten boxes and keys dangling from the locks. "And have a seat."

So far, so good. I could do that. I grabbed the beat-up pen and wrote my name, the date, and the person's name I was visiting. The experience of being here was surreal, but I boldly followed directions and tried to stay strong for Linda and Unkie. I stepped aside and put my backpack inside the locker, gently closed the door, and removed the key, tucking it into my pocket. Linda followed suit, and we both sat in the orange, hard plastic chairs, awaiting to be called back for our visit.

The attendant loudly closed the window and returned to working on her computer. I grabbed Linda's hand and gave it a quick squeeze, continuing to observe the contents of the waiting room. This was not like the lobby of a doctor's office, no magazines present to occupy the time, no soothing background music to ease the waiting time. And there was some type of odor I couldn't place, and frankly, didn't want to.

I didn't know what to expect when we entered through the large gray steel door. There couldn't be much of a space there in little 'ol Belle Harbor. The only vision of jail I had was from TV. From the old west shows, which had just a cell or two, to the massive prisons with multiple stories and acres of cells to house prisoners.

A loud clang startled us as the door leading to the back of the building slowly opened. The attendant had moved from her desk to allow us to enter the next area of the jail. In front of us was a narrow hallway with cubby-hole spaces on our left, the seating areas separated by short dividers for some minuscule amount of privacy between visitors. Each section had two chairs, the same style as those in the lobby, seated together and facing the glass. The woman led us to the second section, gesturing to the seats. "You've got fifteen minutes," she instructed. "I'll give you a five-minute warning. Wait here."

Linda and I both took a seat, facing the glass where I assumed Uncle Jack would soon appear. I smiled at her, hoping to impart some ease for this tense situation. The corners of her mouth struggled to lift up in return. Inhaling deeply, I willed my muscles to relax, holding my stomach as I slowly exhaled.

From around the partition on the other side of the glass, Uncle Jack appeared with a wide grin, dressed in a prison orange jumpsuit. He pulled out the chair and took a seat, looking back and forth between us. "It's so good to see you both," he said through the little speak-through section of the window separating us. He actually didn't look bad at all, just little bags under his eyes. I could only imagine the sleeping quarters were the same type of industrial decor as the waiting and visiting areas.

"Jack," Linda squeaked, reaching out her hand. "Are you OK?"

"I'm fine. The food in here leaves a little something to be desired." He chuckled. Was he just trying to ease our stress or was he really doing OK? "Looking forward to a whole batch of those cream-filled cupcakes all to myself when I'm out of here."

"Uncle Jack, I'm sure you'll be out of here in no time," I said with as much conviction as I could muster. My stomach twisted as I pondered even the slightest possibility that my statement wouldn't come true.

"Of course," he replied. "I know Barney is just doing his job." Unkie and Linda locked eyes. I couldn't fathom my sweetie being locked up and having to visit in this way. The shock of entering this place, let alone the reality of the reason they were in here, was paralyzing.

"Have you talked to Barney?" I looked at Linda, not wanting to monopolize the conversation with the short time we had, but she didn't appear to be in a talkative mood.

Uncle Jack shook his head. "Not much. Which is fine. He's out investigating, which is all good for me."

With Linda still silent, I forged ahead. I had to ask the uncomfortable question weighing me down. "Unkie?" I started.

Still smiling, likely to ease the moment, he appeared to know exactly where my thoughts were going without having to voice them.

"Five minutes left," came the monotone voice over the loudspeaker, jarring all of us.

Linda looked at me, eyes wide, apparently realizing we would soon have to leave. Departing might be harder on her than when we arrived, seeing Uncle Jack behind that wall of glass in a prison jumpsuit.

"Tilly, I wish I had answers," Uncle Jack began as the jail guard came into view, standing with his back against the wall opposite us, ready to whisk Unkie away when the visitation timer expired. Looking at Linda, he continued, "I had gone to check on Clint since we were just about to start the live auction. I'm so sorry you had to see that." Uncle Jack's cheeks drooped, his angst for his love paining his face.

"I'll be OK. We just need to get you out of here," Linda said, sitting up tall. Looking around, she said, "We'll come for another visit as soon as we can." She put her hand on the glass separating the three of us and Uncle Jack mirrored her movement.

With time running out, Uncle Jack finished his explanation. "I stopped in the restroom before seeing Clint. I was finishing up and washing my hands when I heard Linda scream."

The guard behind Unkie stepped forward, the remaining minutes of our visit ticking away. I breathed out, my shoulders relaxing to hear the explanation of the moments just before Clint was discovered. I couldn't figure out how Uncle Jack had gone to find Clint but then the next thing I knew, Linda was screaming as she discovered his body with Uncle Jack's knife protruding from his back and Unkie nowhere to be found. That little piece of the puzzle in place helped to definitively eliminate Uncle Jack as a suspect, at least in my mind.

Now, I needed to figure out a scenario that would place the killer in the right place at the right time, which made Uncle Jack look guilty.

One final step forward from the guard, who put his hand on Uncle Jack's shoulder. He stood and blew us each a kiss as we remained seated, watching him be led away.

CHAPTER SEVEN

The door leading Uncle Jack back to his cell slammed shut, echoing off the bare walls. Linda continued to sit. I reached for her hand as she sobbed, head bowed. "It hurts so much to see him like that," she whimpered.

I stood, bringing her arm up with me, trying to nudge her to follow me. We had to get out of this depressing place as soon as possible. She lifted her head as tears dripped onto her lap, bringing her free arm up to wipe them away. I felt exactly the same way.

"Let's head out to Fiona's. Maybe if we focus on next steps that will make us feel like we're actually helping," I said, trying to convince myself as much as Linda.

She scooted her chair back as the metal legs scraped on the dull gray linoleum floor. We returned to the lobby and retrieved our belongings from the lockers. The attendant opened the window and placed the clipboard on the counter. "Please sign out," she said, handing us a pen.

Silently, Linda and I each wrote our name in the proper column and left the building. As we emerged, a large gust of fresh air hit us as if to wash away the odor and sensation of the jail visit. I breathed deeply to recenter myself and gain my wits about me after that jarring experience. Looking at Linda, I asked, "You OK?"

Nodding, she stepped away from the building, heading down the sidewalk toward Fiona's.

Not knowing how long Unkie would be in jail, I realized I needed to pace my energy, taking one step at a time. The walk to Fiona's would take some time but provided us a chance to burn off some stress. The silence between us was heavy. I just didn't know what to say to improve the situation.

"You know, I think what Uncle Jack said was helpful," I started, unsure if I should completely change the topic to something more neutral.

"How so?" Linda stopped and turned toward me, her short silver hair ruffled by the breeze. She sniffled, her eyes red.

I resumed our walk and began, "Well, we've narrowed down the window of time that the person did this." Our path was taking us down the main street of Belle Harbor along the backside of the shops that bordered the beach. Fiona's bar sat at the end of the row, just before the path continued to the Lighthouse Restaurant and Belle Harbor Park.

"That doesn't seem very helpful," she said.

"I know we want the answer to immediately appear in front of us, but we'll have to take the clues as they come," I said. It wasn't much comfort, but it was the reality of the situation. You couldn't force an answer, but I had learned instead that sometimes you couldn't see the next step until you took the one right in front of you. Continuing, I said, "If we can find out who had gone down that hallway after Uncle Jack and before you, I think we'll be close to solving this." That was a big if. Without security cameras in the place, how would we know people's movements throughout the building? A picture is worth a thousand words, prompting an epiphany.

"Robin!" I exclaimed.

We rounded the corner toward the beach and the entrance to Fiona's.

"What about her?" Linda asked in a snide tone, unlike any response I had seen from her since we had met.

I had to figure out a way to reduce that stress so she and Unkie could enjoy their engagement.

"She was taking pictures at the event for her story in the Belle Harbor Gazette. If we could go through what she has and line them up to the time she took them, we might track the locations of the participants." I bounced on my feet, thrilled with my brainstorm for some actual physical evidence to break this case wide open.

"Maybe," Linda uttered and continued the final steps to Fiona's.

Her half-hearted response stunned me. Why was she not all over my breakthrough idea to find answers? The visit with Uncle Jack must have weighed heavily on her. Fiona would have some good ideas too. We needed all hands on deck to crack this mystery.

Turning the last corner before the entrance to Fiona's, I followed Linda inside. We surveyed the room to locate a small table. In one of the least desirable spots, near the restroom, sat a vacant table for two. The hostess led us to the spot where I hoped to analyze our next steps. Anticipating Fiona could break away for a bit to strategize with us, Linda and I pulled out the wooden chairs and sat as the hostess placed two drink napkins on the table.

"I owe you an apology, Tilly." Linda picked up the menu, her hand trembling, gazing downward.

I reached across the table to grasp her free hand and held tight. "No apology necessary. We will get through this. I'm certain."

Fiona appeared to my left and quietly said, "Hi guys." She dragged a chair from another table and joined us. "How is he?"

Glancing at Linda, I swallowed. Talking about it was as painful as not talking about it. I closed my eyes, seeing Unkie on the other side of the glass divider in the jail visiting area, his smile overtaking his face like normal, even if he was probably putting on a show for us. Always focused on others, like he had been with his volunteer work at the charity auction for the senior dogs. If anything ever happened to him, I vowed to carry on with his work.

"You know Uncle Jack," I replied.

Fiona smiled and nodded. "Of course. He's putting on a brave front for everyone else."

Linda chuckled. "He'd be really upset and annoyed with how I'm letting this get to me. Unnecessarily worrying about him." She sat a little taller and leaned against the back of the chair.

Stacy the server arrived with cold beverages even without us ordering. We made our food selections and all leaned in when she left our table.

Linda started with, "Tilly had a brilliant idea to see if Robin would share pictures from the auction before—"

Rescuing Linda, I explained, "We might be able to put together a more precise timeline and at least eliminate a bunch of people."

Fiona raised her right hand for a high five. "Genius, girl!"

"What I can't figure out is what motive someone would have. Usually if that's clear, I can reverse engineer to suspects," I said. I grabbed my notebook and pen from my backpack to jot down any more details that might come to us.

Fiona glanced toward Linda and back at me as she fidgeted in her chair. What was that about? Linda focused on her silverware wrapped in a paper napkin, picking at the wrapper that held it together.

"What?" I asked, obviously completely missing something between the two of them.

"It's not really Fiona's place to say. And I don't think it means anything . . ." Linda's voice trailed off, not providing any more insight into her behavior.

Fiona sat on her hands as if to help keep her mouth from opening to allow Linda to explain.

With her voice croaking, Linda said, "I used to date Clint." Her head remained down.

I gulped and paused, allowing that revelation to settle enough to process it. Sadly, the outcome was that it provided a crystal-clear motive for Uncle Jack to kill Clint. The oldest in the book: jealousy. The complexity of the case just skyrocketed, along with the urgency to find the actual killer.

CHAPTER EIGHT

The session at Fiona's last night had taken a turn that completely threw me for a loop. Now that I knew Linda and Clint used to date, it was hard for my brain to entertain any other thoughts of who might have a motive to kill Clint. He toured far and wide for his auction business, always pulling in record amounts of money for the organizers. I couldn't see how that would make him a target for murder. And why would someone travel here to do it? In every walk of life there was drama; surely the auction world was no different.

Linda was extra quiet this morning as we accomplished our baking. I wanted to give her peace from discussing the elephant in the room. We sped through our chores, even doubling up a few extra batches of cupcakes for Mocha Joe's special order for his sister's baby shower.

Stepping over to my side as I boxed up the cupcakes for Joe, Linda said, "I know I've been a basket case." She grabbed an empty box to assist with packaging the order.

"It's totally understandable," I said. How could you not be? Did she still have feelings toward Clint? He seemed like an okay guy and actually one that I could see dating Linda. It wasn't my business to pry unless it was pertinent to solving this crime, but I was desperate to know about the conditions of their breakup.

Linda continued, "Clint's traveling was just too much for me." She stopped with the explanation that led me to conclude it was possible she could still have had feelings for him. The complications in this case continued to arrive.

Waiting for any further insight, I held my tongue from quizzing her with the million questions swirling around my brain.

"I would never do anything to hurt Jack," Linda said, folding down the edges of the box she had just filled. "Clint and I parted on good terms, realizing we were just in two different seasons of our lives."

Reminiscing about happy times with Clint must have hurt her, him now murdered and her fiancé accused of the crime. Since she and Clint had parted on good terms, she must also be grieving for him.

I reached in and wrapped Linda in a tight hug, hoping to relieve some of her pain. We continued organizing our supplies for the day, ready for Dexter to arrive to make the deliveries. That kid would put a smile on her face. I grinned just thinking about him, wondering if that's what Uncle Jack would have been like as a teenager. A gregarious kid, focused on making others happy.

"I'm going to head out front and see if we're set with supplies," I said. The normalcy of work was one of the few things keeping me going too. I grabbed a small tub with cleaning cloths to wipe down the tables, sure that I had already done it. The physical labor provided some relief to my stress.

To my delight, Justin was in the lobby heading toward me. He approached and gave me a peck on the cheek, gesturing to a table to sit. "Sorry to arrive unannounced. I couldn't sleep last night worried about you all," he said, glancing toward the kitchen to see if Linda was within earshot. He leaned in, raising his eyebrows.

Where did I start? Startling details were frequently emerging and not in any way leading toward Unkie's exoneration and release from jail. I didn't feel right sharing Linda's relationship history with Justin, but the fact had become a material part of the case.

"Linda and Clint used to date," I blurted.

"Tilly!" Justin replied.

Nodding, I continued, "They parted on good terms, but it clearly provides a motive for Uncle Jack."

"And the murder weapon was Jack's contribution to the auction," Justin added. Sitting back in his seat, he rubbed his chin. Maybe someone not so closely tied to the situation might have a better perspective and be able to assemble the pieces into a different picture. I fiercely banked on that being the case, pinning my hopes on anything I could grasp. Reaching across the table, Justin continued, "We'll figure this out. Please believe that," he pleaded.

I stood, needing to continue the prep work to open the bakery for the usual rush of customers. "I should get back to work," I said.

Following my lead, Justin stood and said, "Of course." Stepping closer to me, he asked in a soft voice, "Do you think we should postpone our date to the comedy club?"

Knowing that would deflate him, and seeing no reason to do so, I shook my head. "Sometimes when I'm unsure what to do, I try to channel Uncle Jack in my head," I said, chuckling.

"You're right," Justin said, gently laying his hand on my arm. "He'd have my hide if we canceled." He looked at his watch. "I can't wait." Quickly rushing in, he hugged me and waved, almost bumping into Jenna as she arrived.

The place was hopping with visitors, all with concern about Linda's and my well-being.

Jenna looked around the lobby, and seeing that we were alone, asked, "How is she?"

I shrugged as I made my way to all the tables, wiping the already cleaned surfaces. "She's OK." What else could I say? She was devastated and her emotions ran the gamut. We would have to take it one moment at a time, that's all we could do.

"Do you think she's still up to visiting the farm today?" Jenna asked. She had offered to take Linda to visit the dogs who were up for adoption by the seniors, funded by the proceeds from the auction that didn't happen.

I moved behind the display counter, placing the cleaning bin on a shelf. "Yes. She's having a hard time doing anything that feels like she's deserting Uncle Jack, but he would insist she go. So she's committed to honoring his wishes."

"That's great. I know for a fact that once she sees those dogs, it will provide some stress therapy," Jenna said.

A loud crash emitted from the kitchen area, followed by raucous laughter from both Linda and Dexter. Apparently, our resident therapy creature himself had arrived to provide some comic relief for Linda. I didn't even care what mess I might find when I entered the kitchen. If it contributed to Linda's load being a little lighter, it was well worth twice the price.

Jenna and I looked at each other and cracked up. "Can't wait. Should we meet you there?" I asked.

I would need to hitch a ride with Linda, as my only mode of transportation was a moped, courtesy of Uncle Jack when I had arrived on his doorstep escaping my former life. That seemed years ago now, and a simpler time I wanted to return to, but there was no going back. The selflessness of that man knew no bounds, and I needed to rally this town around him. If I could enlist them in my quest for the truth, perhaps we could expedite his release, and the capture of the actual murderer who continued to be free.

CHAPTER NINE

Even before arriving at the farm with the dogs, my stress level was reducing. The drive to Oakey Dokey Acres wound us through centuries-old Evergreen trees on a two-lane country road. Periodically, the scenery would open to fields of crops for acres and then plunge us again into overgrown trees. I rolled down the window a crack to inhale the fresh air and instead got a whiff of the cow farm we had just passed.

Chuckling at the irony, I hoped Jenna was right and this trip would snap Linda out of her well-deserved funk. Truthfully, I needed the canine therapy too. Would there be a dog in my future? My little kitten was an indoor creature and fairly self-sufficient. A dog would be a whole other level of responsibility, but as I was told, well worth it. Maybe someday, but for now, just me and my little Peanut.

Linda slowed the car as we came upon a tractor motoring down the road. She drifted into the opposite lane and passed the farm equipment, the driver raising his hand in a greeting. This certainly appeared to be a slower life, away from the hustle and bustle of town. Despite the manure odor, the sounds of the country were just about as soothing as that of the ocean waves. A jaunt to the country would be fine, but I didn't see how I could ever move from my proximity to the beach.

Seeing the sign for Oakey Dokey Acres up ahead, Linda turned on her blinker and said, "Tilly, I just want to thank you for being a rock. I know this isn't easy for you either. And I really appreciate your strength through this."

I am glad she thinks I'm a rock, because on the inside I'm Jell-O. "Of course," I replied. I might break down someday, but for now I didn't have that luxury. Plus, my mission to find the killer occupied my mind.

We ambled down the gravel driveway toward an opening near a barn. Jenna's car was already here with a couple of others, which must have belonged to either employees or volunteers. Linda pulled alongside Jenna's car and turned off the ignition, looking at me. "I'm done wallowing in pity. I'm determined to join you in finding the murderer and freeing Jack." She curtly nodded and reached for the door handle to exit the car.

Stepping outside the car, we heard barking coming from around the side of the barn. Looking at Linda, I pointed, and we made our way to the dog kennel. Rounding the corner, we discovered quite a luxurious lodging for those dogs. There were about ten dogs, each who had their own little house and kennel. The houses had blankets inside, with food and water in the kennel. Each kennel led to a large open area that had play and exercise equipment to entertain the dogs. At the far end was a swimming pool. These guys had it made.

Raising her hand in greeting, Jenna approached and swung her arm around. "What do you think?" she asked.

"It's quite something," Linda replied.

"These guys are treated well, as they should be," Jenna said, turning and heading toward the open yard. "Let's go meet a couple of them."

I knew little about dog breeds, but it looked like there were a variety of what I would call small- to medium-sized dogs. Every single one of them appeared to be smiling ear to ear.

We followed Jenna as she entered through a gate and were swarmed by the dogs. They approached, and each sat in front of us, well trained, waiting for the next command.

"Can I pet one?" Linda asked, reaching out her arm to a wiggly brown and white long-furred critter.

"Yes. We've trained them to wait for permission, since they will live with elderly individuals. We don't want them to accidentally topple one of them over in their exuberance," Jenna explained.

Linda crouched and let the little one closest to her approach and lick her face. Giggling, she said, "I want to take them all home with me."

"That's usually the reaction we get from visitors," Jenna said as she bent to scratch the ears of the dog closest to her.

I followed suit and joined in the greeting, one arm for each of the two closest to me. I might just have to make some spare time to volunteer at this place. I could see why it was so close to Uncle Jack's heart.

"Aren't they all adorable?" said a familiar voice behind me.

Standing, I turned to find Robin with her camera in front of her, quickly snapping an excessive number of pictures. Perfect! I would seize the opportunity to ask her about seeing those she took the night of the auction. She might even thank me for the suggestion that could lead to a an award for her reporting if she was instrumental in finding the killer.

"What a pleasant surprise. I'm glad you're here," I said.

Letting the camera drop from her hands and dangle from the strap around her neck, she replied, "Why?"

Furrowing my brow, I paused, taken aback at her response. Who wouldn't want to be greeted that way? And why would she adopt such a defensive stance? "I had a brainstorm about finding clues to Clint's murder."

Glancing at Linda to make sure I hadn't upset her with the abrupt change in conversation, I saw she continued to immerse herself in the canine reception. So far, so good with the mission to reduce her stress.

Stepping back from the group, Robin stared, not saying a word.

I guided her away and quietly said, "I think if I can look at your pictures and the timing, I might make a list of suspects based on process of elimination."

Her jaw set, she spoke through almost gritted teeth. "My editor wouldn't allow it."

"Even just to look?" From my peripheral vision, I saw Linda and Jenna retrieving toys to play with the dogs, giving me a bit more time to quiz Robin. "I don't want to take anything."

"Nope. Can't do it. If they are as valuable as you think, the police may want them first," she suggested.

Yes, that's what I thought. I was only hoping I could get there first. Once Barney inserted his official protocol, they would be off-limits to me. "Well, can you at least check with your editor? I'm happy to review them together with you both." What could I say to negotiate this in my favor?

"And this is an open investigation, anyway." Robin jerked her head in Linda's direction. "She might just have to spend the rest of her life visiting Jack behind bars." Her cheeks flushed. "That would be tragic," she said, returning to Jenna and Linda and resuming her photography.

Did Robin have some independent investigation going on? Was there some evidence that further implicated Uncle Jack that she wasn't disclosing? What could it be? No way was he involved, but sometimes twisting the truth could present a very different picture from reality. I was not expecting to feel worse than when I arrived, but the interaction with Robin made me feel sick.

CHAPTER TEN

Keeping Linda centered on anything but Uncle Jack's situation today took all of my energy. She was quite enamored by the visit to the farm, and I was eternally grateful for Jenna's suggestion to see the dogs. Linda's focus for now was on the future with Unkie, even pondering the possibility of them adopting a dog after they were married. I was convinced he would do anything to make her happy. That was my dear uncle. Now there was only the minor detail of solving Clint's murder to ensure their blissful future together.

The bakery routine was business as usual today. Going through the motions, I worked hard to keep my plans for the afternoon a secret. Another visit to Uncle Jack in jail so soon might cause Linda to regress, and I couldn't jeopardize that. Plus, I hoped to catch Barney for an unofficial chat. He humored me in my amateur sleuthing, although there had been a time or two when I had uncovered key evidence for him to arrest other criminals. I think he secretly appreciated my efforts, but publicly he couldn't be seen tolerating interference.

I pushed open the door to the lobby leading to the jail. The same attendant from my prior visit was behind the glass, lifting her head as I arrived. She slid the window halfway and asked, "Are you here to see Jack?"

Nodding, I said, "Yes, but first, is Barney in?" Would he even agree to see me? Would it appear as a conflict of interest in the investigation of his best friend?

The attendant leaned back in her chair, stretching her neck to the left and peering down the hallway. "His door is open. Let me see." She disappeared.

Dropping my backpack from my shoulder, I prepared to place it in a locker as I had the previous visit to see Uncle Jack.

Returning to the window and sliding it all the way open, she said, "Yes, he's in." She rounded her desk, opening the door to my left. "Follow me."

Trailing the woman, we quietly filed down the hallway, lined with photos on both sides with former police chiefs and awards. Stopping, she extended her arm toward the opening to Barney's office.

"Thank you," I said, watching her return to her post. I supposed there was no harm in her overhearing my conversation, so I left the door open.

"Tilly." Barney raised up from his desk, coming around it to hug me, his eyebrows raised as he extended his arms, staring at me.

Knowing what he wanted, I shrugged and dropped into the chair facing his desk. "She's OK. Probably as good as she could be," I said, reporting on the well-being of Linda as I knew it.

Returning to his chair, Barney said, "This is extremely hard on everyone. I have had to let my deputy take the lead in the investigation since I'm so close to Jack." Barney's voice cracked. It hadn't even occurred to me how he must be feeling in this situation. He and Uncle Jack were like brothers. And when Uncle Frank passed, Barney's presence steadied Unkie as he processed his grief.

"I'm so sorry Barney. I know you can't share with me, but I may have a brainstorm that could help. Though, it's possible you already have this covered," I said, sitting up in my chair, hopeful I could bring light and progress to hasten the resolution to the murder.

Slowly nodding, Barney smiled. "I can always count on you, Tilly. For better or worse," he said.

"It might be nothing," I said, "But I have to try, with Unkie's future on the line."

"What have you got?" Barney asked, hands clasped in front of him on the desk. In his line of work, you probably couldn't get too excited about one piece of evidence until you verified its credibility.

"Well," I started, placing my backpack on my lap and hugging it. This was the moment of truth. My idea would either be brilliant and advance the case or be wildly irrelevant, with no bearing on the outcome. Closing my eyes and forging ahead, I said, "Robin was at the auction taking pictures, right?"

"Yes," Barney replied.

Continuing, I studied his expression to see how this would land. "What I wondered was, could we look at those and create a timeline of who was where to see if we could narrow down the list of suspects?" I paused, my idea now in full display.

Shaking his head and looking down, Barney said, "Tilly, you never cease to amaze me."

What kind of response was that, and where was he going with it? My heart dropped to my stomach as I resigned to the fact my suggestion was not worthy enough to help solve the murder. Either they had already done it, or it was a dumb idea. But Robin had mentioned no other requests she had received to look at the pictures. Goosebumps raised on my arms; this had to be helpful.

"First, it can't be *we*," he said. Of course not. Officially, I was not on the law-enforcement team.

"Sorry. I misspoke," I said, fully willing to give credit to Barney or his deputy. But what did he think of the idea? He was slow walking me to his response.

Grinning and standing up, he said, "I must be way too close to this." He chuckled, leaning against his desk in front of me. "That's a brilliant idea. And I don't think Deputy Stevens even thought of that yet." His expression brightened the room.

I exhaled, not realizing I had been holding my breath waiting for his response.

He returned to the back of his desk and picked up his phone, informing Deputy Stevens that he needed to contact the newspaper editor to request access to Robin's photos. Hanging up, he raised his arm in the air as a victory salute. Not wanting to be too optimistic yet, I would wait for the results of that analysis.

With a bounce in his step, Barney asked, "Did you just come to see me? Or are you visiting Jack too?"

I stood. "Both. Is that OK?" I asked, heading toward the door.

"The old codger could use some good news," Barney chided. "Although his attitude throughout this entire thing has been commendable." Barney escorted me back to the lobby for the screening process before I could enter the prisoner visiting area.

The incongruity of the word prisoner in the same breath as Uncle Jack made my head hurt. Placing my backpack in the locker, I slowed my movements so that my news to Unkie could be delivered in a measured manner not to get his hopes up. Though, how could you not be more optimistic? I signed my name on the visitor log, and the attendant released the latch on the door leading to the visitor hallway. Sadly, I was getting the routine down for prisoner visitations. I entered the hallway and proceeded to the third cubicle this time, ready to share an update with Unkie. I rounded the privacy wall to discover him seated with the goofiest grin plastered on his face. So much life learning still remained for me to glean from that guy. Oh, how I loved him.

CHAPTER ELEVEN

I couldn't help but mirror his expression, and perhaps that was his motive. Scooting the plastic chair back from the counter, I sat with my hands clasped in my lap.

"Tilly, thank you for coming. But you don't have to do this. I'm going to be just fine," Uncle Jack said, leaning forward with his elbows on the opposite counter, his bushy beard settled into his hands.

"I know. Just keeping you up to date," I replied. Would I get weary of visiting if this situation continued to drag on? What if it were weeks or months? It was certainly possible, but I couldn't let that happen, and I was in this for the long haul, no matter what.

"You're too busy with work. And I'm not worried, so you shouldn't be either," he continued, tipping his head.

Oh, I wanted to hug him so badly. Was there any way Barney would let me in for just one second so that I could be enveloped in an Unkie bear hug? I wrapped my arms around myself.

"And I know you want to hear about Linda. She's coping," I started. How much should I reveal? No doubt hearing how Linda was struggling would severely dampen Unkie's demeanor. "Pretty busy with work. And we went to the farm to see the dogs."

He leaned back in his chair. "And?"

I laughed. "I think you have a dog in your future. And speaking of future, you'll get a big kick out of this."

The door to Uncle Jack's right opened up, and the guard entered. "Ten-minute warning," he barked and exited the room.

Feeling a need to speed through the rest of my updates, I blurted out, "Carlos and Annie had their baby."

Uncle Jack clapped his hands. "And?" He was practically bouncing in his chair.

"It actually happened right in your store," I began. There was so much more to the story. "Florence had come by because a customer had forgotten a package. Just as she was handing it to the lady, Annie went into labor."

Unkie's hand flew to his mouth. Little did he know this was going to be an epic story told for the ages.

"Florence stepped right up and helped deliver the baby until the medics arrived."

Uncle Jack stood and began pacing. "That blows my mind. Are you sure?" he asked, returning to his seat. If even for just a little I was thrilled to distract him from the fact he was in jail, accused of murdering his fiancé's former boyfriend.

"Mom, dad, baby, and Florence are all doing well," I said.

"Wow, I'm just stunned. Sorry I missed it," he uttered.

"And the best part. They named him Jack."

Unkie's chin slightly quivered. There wasn't much that fazed that guy, but this did it. Unable to speak, he shook his head, wiping his eye with the back of his hand. "Can't wait to meet him," he said.

"I also just came from checking in with Barney. We've got an idea that might help solve the case." I didn't want to bring him false hope, but this might be the beginning of the end of his time in the joint.

"We?" he said, chuckling.

"Ha ha. You sound exactly like Barney. And no way I'm keeping my nose out of this until you're free." I scooted closer to the glass, excited for my idea to play out. "Remember how Robin was taking pictures the night of the auction?"

Unkie nodded. "Yeah, she was everywhere."

"Well," I continued, "I think if we could look at them and put together a timeline of who was where at what time, we could at least narrow down the list of suspects." Staring at Unkie, I hoped for a positive response to the suggestion.

"Hmmm," he mumbled. What was he thinking? The killer was one of the attendees. Did he know more about any suspects than he was letting on? Why wouldn't he provide a theory so he could get himself out of here?

"It could help, right? Barney's going to talk to the editor to get a copy of the pictures," I said. Why didn't he seem more excited? This could crack the case wide open.

"Unkie?" I prompted. His body remained still as if he was pondering my news. Maybe he just didn't want to get his hopes up. I got that this was the most progress yet, and I was desperate for any inkling of a break in the case.

"I'll believe it when I see it," he said.

Fair enough, but that turn toward negativity was diametrically opposed to the constantly uplifting person I knew.

"What's your concern?" I asked. If I needed to temper my enthusiasm, I wanted to understand why. What was he not telling me?

"I'll give it to you that the killer was at the auction. However, the murder weapon belonged to me. And with Linda and Clint previously dating . . ." he trailed off. Yes, the jealousy motive was a central factor, but the man in front of me was no more jealous of Clint than he was the King of England.

"Yes, she told me, but they ended the relationship on friendly terms," I pleaded.

"Tilly, your idea about Robin's pictures was brilliant. And I hope it works out, but I can't get too excited yet for something that may not happen."

"Do you have any idea who might have done this?" I was sure he had been wracking his brain nonstop since the arrest. If he wasn't able to identify any suspects, he might just be in here a while longer.

He shook his head. "Let's change the subject." The air in the room felt heavy and the clock on the wall ticked over to exactly ten minutes since the guard had warned us about the end of the visit. I glanced toward the door, expecting our visit would be halted until next time. "What have you and Justin been up to?" he asked, always focused on the well-being of others above himself.

My face warmed and I lowered my eyes. Uncle Jack read me like a book. "We actually have our first official date tonight," I said, wiggling in my chair like a nervous little schoolgirl. Hurrying my explanation for fear we would get cut off mid-sentence by the guard's interruption, I continued, "We're going for drinks and to a comedy club in Diamond Hills."

"Tilly, thank you," Unkie said.

I furrowed my brow, confused by that response.

He added, "It makes me so happy that you are not putting your life on hold while I'm in here."

The door admitting the guard opened and Uncle Jack stood, our visit being terminated. What did that comment mean? Did he have some reason to believe he would be in here longer than we all assumed? I stood as he was escorted away by the guard, blowing him a kiss, tears filling my eyes.

CHAPTER TWELVE

Justin grabbed my hand as we joined the line to enter the Chortles Comedy Club to watch the evening's improv group. The guilt settled into my body, as all I could think about was freeing Uncle Jack. The best way to do that was to prove he had an airtight alibi or find the person responsible, or at least a viable suspect. How could I enjoy myself when I felt I should spend every waking moment investigating details?

Squeezing my hand as we slowly navigated toward the front door, Justin said, "Tilly, it's OK to take a break. To take some time for yourself."

I looked up at him, curly blond hair slightly waving in the breeze. He had put pants on for our date tonight—one of the few times I hadn't seen him wearing his board shorts.

Shaking my head, I said, "I can't help it."

"Actually, I think giving your brain a break might help you see things differently," he said.

I knew he was right, but that didn't make it any easier. "I just get so frustrated when the answer is front and center and I'm not seeing it," I replied. The killer was at the auction, but who was it? I doubted I would have the opportunity to see those pictures from Robin, so I just had to hope that Barney's deputy did his job thoroughly. Pulling out my phone, I started to text Barney.

Justin put his hand on my arm. "That doesn't look like you're taking a break," he said.

I dropped my arms and tucked my phone into a pocket in my backpack. "I just had a thought I wanted Barney to pass along to Deputy Stevens," I said quietly. "I promise to focus on the show when it starts." I looked up at Justin, more guilt consuming me for the distractions taking me away from being present on our first official date. I couldn't win.

"I think you should text him so you won't be agonizing about it the entire night," he suggested, his mouth stretching wide into a knowing smile.

"Thank you for understanding. I really want to see Robin's pictures, but I don't think that's going to happen," I said, retrieving my phone and tapping out a quick message to Barney, certain he would shake his head when he received my note. I couldn't care about what others thought right now with my sole focus on liberating my uncle.

Justin showed our tickets to the person at the door as we entered the darkened room. We scanned for an open table, finding a two-seater along the left side. Music blared over the loudspeaker as servers visited tables gathering drink orders. The stage was spotlighted with a micro-phone on a stand in the center, waiting for the opening act. The show had one stand-up comedian, then an improv group of four would perform the main act. This type of fun would have been beneath what my ex would consider entertainment, and for that reason alone, I was all in. How could you not enjoy something specifically designed to make you laugh?

Justin held out my chair, then gently nudged it in as I sat, briefly placing his hand on my shoulder. I closed my eyes and laid my hand on his. Moving to the opposite side of the table, he pulled out the menus and handed one to me. "What would you like?"

We scanned the options and provided our choices to the server that appeared to take our order. I glanced at the stage, ready for this distraction. Looking at Justin, I said, "Thank you for asking me out. This was a great idea."

"Thank you for saying yes." He chuckled. Leaning in, he said, "Secretly, I've always wanted to be a comedian."

I sat back in my chair, trying to imagine this relaxed guy up on stage regaling crowds with frivolity. "You should come to open mic night sometime," I suggested.

I grinned from ear to ear, and if I wasn't mistaken, he was slightly blushing.

"You already have, haven't you?" I asked as the server arrived with our drinks and appetizers. Waiting for her departure, I continued, "Why didn't you say something? I would have come to cheer you on."

He snagged a few mozzarella sticks for his plate and nibbled the end of one to avoid answering my question. Munching down, and looking around, he said, "OK. Let's change the subject." He fidgeted in his chair. I would not let this go, vowing there would be return visits to the comedy club for open mic night. "There's not long before the show starts. How about we sleuth as much as possible before then so you can enjoy the show when it begins?"

This guy got me as much as Uncle Jack did, knowing what I needed, maybe even more than I realized. Nodding, I pulled out my trusty chart and pen so we could quickly make our notes.

"I feel like I'm at the end of my knowledge," I said, making a circle in the middle of the page with Clint's name inside. "Let's start fresh and maybe you can provide some suggestions to see how this plays out." I drew multiple lines from Clint's circle toward the outer edge of the page, connecting to empty circles. Even filling only one of them with a name other than Unkie or Linda would give me some relief.

"I've been thinking about what you said about Robin's pictures, trying to remember who was where just before we heard Linda's screams," Justin started. The stage preparations had begun to set up for the first act, and assistants placed a stool and a water bottle on top, next to the microphone stand. The person on stage said, "Testing, 1-2-2," into the microphone.

I looked down, pen poised, as my hopes soared with possibilities of new suspects entering the picture, no matter how remotely far from the crime they might seem.

"I was standing on the side of the room next to the surfboard where I could see down the hallway that led to the restrooms," Justin continued as he grabbed another cheese stick.

He better be going somewhere with this, or my night might just be ruined. "OK. If you close your eyes and put yourself back there, what do you see?"

His eyelids dropped, and he smiled. "I don't know his name, but there was a guy returning from the hallway, taller than me, older, dark hair." He opened his eyes. "Sorry, that's all I've got."

I popped up straight in my chair, writing Justin's details on my paper. "That might just be it."

"I didn't know the guy, but sometimes these auctions draw people from outside Belle Harbor. I know they advertise far and wide to get the most exposure," he said as the lights on the stage brightened.

Justin's epiphany might just be the smallest crack in the case leading to a big break. This night was turning out to be the best one in quite a while. Justin turned his chair to face the stage, looking back at me over his shoulder, smiling. I would wait until tomorrow to text Barney. Nothing was going to happen at this late hour. And Justin deserved my full attention for this date.

CHAPTER THIRTEEN

The multi-purpose room at the Whispering Palms Retirement Community was filled with residents and guests for the presentation ceremony. Without the funds raised from the charity auction, the annual adoption of the dogs by the seniors had been postponed, and it was doubtful whether it would occur. Jenna let Linda and I know that an anonymous donor had made up the difference that the auction would have provided, and then some, so that the adoption could proceed. The dogs we had met at the farm were positioned up front near a speaker's podium, well-behaved and decked out in colorful neckerchiefs. Jenna and a helper had them seated side by side like little soldiers at attention. The residents were milling about, the excitement palpable.

Whispering Palms would be a place I would like to live in my twilight years if I was by myself. The residential setup provided many choices for living, whether in a small single-family home, in an apartment, or a room in the main complex for those who needed more help and frequent care. The facility provided numerous amenities to support the active older adults, including a park exclusively for use by those with dogs.

"Hi Robin, this is incredible," I said, sweeping my arm around as Linda and I approached the sherbet serving station.

Robin had been whispering with the man providing the sherbet when we arrived. "Um, yeah. This is great," she stuttered, stepping away from the table, her ever-present camera strapped around her neck. That still might be the only key to unlock the mystery of Clint's killer.

Linda and I each picked up a small bowl with a scoop of lime sherbet and stepped away from the table. One dog had escaped Jenna's grasp and made a beeline toward us, stretching a tongue up toward a bowl of sherbet. Those little pups deserved all of that and more. Jenna's helper scurried to retrieve the wayward dog and return it to the front, where the presentation was about to begin.

Moving right next to Linda, Robin said, "Too bad Jack isn't here." She pulled up her camera, snapping several pictures of the room, stepping back and taking one of Linda and me standing at the sherbet station.

Linda scooped a small amount of the frozen dessert into her mouth, averting her eyes from Robin. That was a low blow, Robin. But I guess as a reporter you had to go straight at the subject to get the story, sticking your nose into other people's business.

"Maybe we should be seated. It looks like they might be getting ready to start," I suggested, trying to ease the tension of the situation as another dog had escaped in our direction.

I crouched to receive him in my arms to keep him from the sherbet.

"I feel like we're all safer with him in jail, though. Right, Linda?" Robin continued. Now she was just being mean. I wouldn't blame Linda for decking her for that comment.

Holding the dog's bandanna until they could retrieve him, I scooted between Linda and Robin to try to avoid an incident.

"Yes, Tilly. Let's grab a seat," Linda said, striding forward.

Glaring at Robin as I released the dog to Jenna, I followed Linda, preparing for some damage control. There was no excuse for the additional pain Robin was causing.

Linda had taken a seat about midway toward the front of the room, separate from any others. I suspected people didn't know what to say to her, so they avoided any conversation. Closing my eyes, I wished with all my heart that the actual killer would soon be identified and allow everyone to put all of this behind us.

"Tilly," came Barney's gentle voice and touch on my elbow. "You OK?"

I jumped, putting my hand on my heart. "Barney," was all I said. The question on the tip of my tongue wouldn't budge. I was torn between wanting to know the answer and scared it wouldn't be what I wanted. Forcing it out, I asked, "Did you get a chance to look at Robin's pictures from the auction?" Glancing over my shoulder at Linda, I gestured to Barney to move out of earshot.

He nodded, stepping to the side of the room and away from anyone else.

My pulse raced, my breath shallow as he answered, "We did. I'm letting Deputy Stevens follow up." Scanning around, he continued, softly saying, "I just don't know, Tilly."

I wanted answers, and the only one I would entertain was the evidence to free Uncle Jack. Daring to clarify his comment, I asked, "So nothing there provided any other suspects?"

"Deputy Stevens is doing the detailed analysis of them. And he still has a lot of interviews to complete," Barney replied.

Dejected, I concluded that Uncle Jack would be in jail for quite a while longer. How in the world would Linda handle this? I couldn't break the news to her during this joyous occasion. There would apparently be plenty of time after this to share the discouraging report.

Joining us near the wall, Robin greeted Barney and continued snapping pictures of the festivities from this new vantage point. Was she attempting to eavesdrop on any information she could report in the newspaper about the murder? Moving from Barney's side over to my right, she continued photographing but only focused on Linda, who continued to sit alone. Robin departed toward the front of the room, her camera poised in front of her face, still pointed in Linda's direction.

I glanced around to see what else she might be capturing in her photos, assuming the subjects would include the adopting residents and their new dogs. Jenna had moved the dogs to the left side of the seating area as the announcer was approaching the podium. Robin quickly turned and snapped a picture of the retirement community administrator and took a few steps toward the corner, still focused in Linda's direction.

"Ladies, gentleman, and canines," came the announcement. "I am Colleen O'Brien, the director of community relations for the Whispering Palms Retirement Community." The crowd migrated to the seats as the dogs got fidgety, as if sensing the highlight of their day was near. Jenna and her helper crouched and put their arms around the dogs to calm them, albeit a somewhat futile effort.

Continuing the welcome remarks, Colleen said, "I couldn't be happier that we can have this annual adoption event, thanks to an anonymous donor saving the day." She paused, the air heavy as we all filled in the unsaid words about the auction and the murder. Uncle Jack would be front and center for this occasion every year, and his absence was unmistakable. I hoped this would be the only year he would ever be missing. It just had to be. Barney and I had taken seats next to Linda, and I grabbed her hand as Colleen finished her opening remarks.

The front row of seats held the lucky recipients of this year's adoption, and the delight on their faces mirrored the exuberance of the dogs they were about to receive.

Robin stepped out of the corner, her camera pointed directly at us.

CHAPTER FOURTEEN

"Jenna." Colleen gestured for her to join her at the front. "Let's get on with the show."

Jenna had leashed up each dog for an easier handling of them by their new owners. Holding the leash of the first dog, she led the small curly-haired, light brown dog to the front. Colleen asked for the first resident to approach them and receive their new companion. The happiness of both parties in the adoption was over the top, the resident taking the leash from Jenna, who reached to pick up the dog. The resident closed her eyes and hugged the wiggly little one tight to her chest. I wished I had a recording of this to share with Uncle Jack. Despite his absence, the legacy of his passion project would live on long past him. As the first resident turned to return to her seat, Robin stepped forward for more event photos. Strangely, she was not focused on the adoptive duo, but remained concentrated on Linda.

I slightly turned my head toward Linda to see if she had noticed Robin's behavior, and what seemed to be an inordinate number of pictures directed at her. Thankfully, Linda's attention remained on the reason for the ceremony, as it should be. Her heart must be as heavy as mine with the obvious absence of the one who was responsible for this adoption program.

Jenna returned to the side of the room and took the leash of the second dog to be going to a new home. The pug, with a wrinkly, short-muzzled face and curly tail, wiggled all the way up to the podium. Colleen gestured for the second resident to join them and receive their new friend. Robin looked their direction, snapped a few times with the camera and pivoted back toward Linda.

This was getting weird, and I couldn't figure out why. Being the center of attention was always uncomfortable for me, so any surveillance was especially noticeable. Colleen and Jenna continued the introductions of the next human and canine to be united. From the corner of my eye, I saw Robin perform the same action of quick shots of the front of the room, then return her camera's focus to Linda.

I shifted my left elbow just enough to touch Barney's arm. Leaning toward me, still watching the front of the room, he asked, "Yes?"

Placing my hand on my knee so it would be out of sight from Robin, I pointed in her direction. Certainly, being in law enforcement, I expected Barney's powers of observation to at least be in sync with mine and discern Robin's motive for her obsession over photographing Linda. Instead, he appeared to be consumed in the moment, which is where I should have been. I bit my tongue to restrain any instinct to interrupt this beautiful presentation, but my gut was directing me otherwise. It couldn't be. How could I have missed the obvious for this long? If I needed to make a scene to save Uncle Jack and spring him from jail, so be it.

"Robin," was all I said to Barney.

Turning his head to look at me, he furrowed his brow. I guess that was a pretty cryptic statement.

"Robin," I quietly repeated.

Barney's eyes widened, clicking with the message I was sending. Finally, dude.

"Do you really think so?" he asked.

All the other explanations I had contorted in my brain to figure out who could have killed Clint never fit all the criteria. While Unkie certainly was accused of having a jealousy motive because of Linda's former relationship with Clint, along with the opportunity to be in the same location near the time of the murder. And the final straw for the case was the murder weapon he had donated to the auction. Strictly by the book, Unkie would go away for a lifetime.

"The only person not in Robin's pictures was Robin," I said. Since she was behind the camera, it was almost as if she was invisible to the investigation, only her photos to be considered a resource for evidence.

Glancing our direction, Linda tilted her head, her mouth opening and closing, absent any words coming out.

I shivered. Linda, Barney, and I all looked Robin's direction as she suddenly dropped the camera to allow it to dangle from the strap. She glanced toward the front of the room and took a small step toward the door.

Colleen and Jenna kept the group's attention with the next greeting of the wiggliest dog of all, a chestnut and white floppy-eared, stout little Cavalier Kings Charles Spaniel. I wished we could avoid the commotion, but there was no way we could not disrupt this ceremony with Robin's takedown. Her preoccupation with Linda was unnatural and must have come from jealousy of Linda's relationship with Uncle Jack. Reflecting back to Robin's interest in their engagement and photographing them for the announcement in the newspaper, I was certain she should be the suspect front and center in Clint's murder. If she couldn't have Uncle Jack, she would frame him for the murder and ensure Linda wouldn't have him either.

Taking two baby steps toward the door, Robin scanned the room.

Scooting to the edge of my chair, I stretched my right leg out, ready to spring from the aisle.

Robin was nearing the door, moments away from escape. She removed the camera strap from around her neck and tucked it under her arm as she turned to exit the room.

Glancing back at me, Linda turned and lunged toward Robin, grabbing her and tackling her to the ground. Squirming, Robin screamed, "Get off of me. Barney, arrest her for assault."

Linda kept Robin's arms pinned to the floor as they both writhed more than the adoptees had when they met their new humans.

Barney rose and pulled his handcuffs from his jacket pocket and grabbed Robin's arm, releasing her from Linda's grasp.

"What are you doing?" Robin screamed.

"I'm arresting you for the murder of Clint Harshman," Barney replied, reading her rights.

Linda stood, and I enveloped her in a hug as she sobbed.

Barney led Robin from the room as she continued to profess her innocence and make a scene, blaming Uncle Jack for his jealousy. With her voice echoing down the hall, Robin yelled, "You don't deserve him."

Linda buried her head on my shoulder as the room remained silent. We returned to our seats so Linda could gather herself and the presentations could conclude. So many stories to share with Unkie when we finally got to celebrate his release.

CHAPTER FIFTEEN

The sun sank into the ocean horizon, creating a combined palette of shades competing between amber and blue. Unkie and Linda sat on the porch swing of his deck overlooking Belle Harbor, gently swaying, hands tightly clasped with each other. I suspected the little cocoon of this space was one that they might never want to leave. With the recent events reminding everyone that circumstances can change on a dime and may be out of your control, you must cherish moments with the ones you love. Though, as usual, Uncle Jack had put us at ease about his time in jail, always one for adventure and finding the best in every situation, even incarceration. That man could give classes in attitude adjustment. When the situation looked dire, Uncle Jack kept his head up and was the guiding light for all around him to have faith it would work out.

Uncle Jack's kitten, Pancake, had grown enough to notice a change during the time he had been in jail. The little fur ball sat on Linda's lap, purring so loudly I could hear him from where I sat. Everyone was relieved to finally have the mystery of Clint's death solved.

Uncle Jack broke the silence. "Thank you, Tilly."

Turning my head, I smiled at the serene view of the three of them as a family.

"I just asked myself, what would Uncle Jack do?" I chuckled, setting my drink glass on the side table. I suspected his gratitude was for my support of Linda through this harrowing ordeal. It must have killed him that he wasn't able to comfort her. And no doubt he would spend the rest of his life making up for that, this nightmare bringing them even closer together.

Linda leaned her head on Unkie's shoulder and closed her eyes, the swing continuing to lightly rock.

"And this one here—" He gestured toward Linda. "Remind me never to argue with her," he said quietly as Linda smiled, her eyes still closed. "Robin never had a chance with my two favorite ladies teaming up."

After Barney had escorted Robin from the retirement community, she had sung like a little birdie, trying to justify her actions and blame Linda for everything. It turned out that she had been jealous of Linda for quite some time and had used her position as a newspaper reporter to spy on her. Robin's strategy had worked well to integrate her into Uncle Jack and Linda's lives, pretending like she was interested in them. We may never know if her killing of Clint was a well-planned scheme or just a spur-of-the-moment decision prompted by her rage at seeing Unkie and Linda together.

"I tell you one thing. I'm ready to get back to the shop," Uncle Jack said. "Changing up my daily routine was the toughest part. Who knew I was a creature of such habit?"

"Yeah, there is something reassuring about the every day. Though, has there ever been ordinary in your life or at Checkered Past Antiques?" I asked. I was certain Uncle Jack would have kept his cool when Annie went into labor in his shop. What he couldn't keep cool about was how Florence had jumped right in and took control of the birth. When we finally gave him the play-by-play of how that all went down, he was in tears, laughing so hard he couldn't speak.

Pancake stood, stretched, and leaped onto the deck, ambling in my direction for another lap and set of hands for petting. I snagged him and hugged him, grateful for the batch of kittens that had also provided me with my very own companion at home. My little Peanut.

"Did you find out yet who the anonymous donor was for the dog adoption?" We all speculated who it might be, but the way the money was provided made it hard to confirm. If not for that generous person, those lovely dogs and seniors might have had to wait another year for the fundraising auction. Though the current auction was being re-scheduled for next month, it would have been agony to delay the annual event that brought boundless joy for all involved.

"I have my suspicions it was Florence," Unkie offered.

Nodding, I said, "Me too. I tried to grill Barney, but he just grinned and mimed locking his lips and throwing away the key."

When we first met Florence, she had purchased the space next to Unkie's shop with plans to open a bookstore. At the time, she had put on airs, indicating with her last name of Kennedy that she was related to the famous Kennedy clan. She seemed pretty full of herself, so we chalked it up to ego, and it was easy enough to make that claim with that last name. With the revelation of the donation, Florence's claim might just have some validity after all.

"Yeah, with his job, he's pretty good at keeping mum when he needs to," Uncle Jack said. "No doubt he was threatened to keep his mouth shut."

Linda lifted her head and tapped Unkie on his knee. "Hey." Barney and Florence as a couple still didn't compute to us. From an outsider's view, they were quite opposite. But early on, we learned about Barney's love of classic literature, and that commonality between them generated a spark that seemed to grow brighter all the time.

"You know, Jack. We have plans to make." Linda gazed lovingly up at Unkie.

"I'm all in," he replied.

I sat forward as Pancake jumped up, stretched, and returned to Linda and Unkie.

"I've been thinking about locations," Linda started.

And I was sure when Uncle Jack said he was all in that there would be nothing Linda could suggest that he wouldn't do.

"While I love living in Belle Harbor with the tropical weather and scenery, I am thinking about something different for the ceremony."

"Hmmm, OK." Uncle Jack looked at me and shrugged.

I mirrored his gesture, not having a clue where Linda was going with this.

"What do you think about snow?" she asked.

"It sounds cold," he replied, chuckling.

"I would love a destination wedding at a winter resort. It sounds so romantic in a lodge with a roaring fire, snow outside," Linda said.

Uncle Jack turned and kissed her cheek. "That sounds perfect. I would follow you to the ends of the earth, my darling." This wedding was going to be epic.

WHAT'S NEXT? BISCOTTI AND BETRAYAL

Waylaid wedding plans, harrowing backyard hobbies, and the wildest chase of her life...

Tenth in the Belle Harbor Cozy Mystery series!

Tilly's exploration of quaint Belle Harbor has taken her on many adventures with her new love. Hiking high upon the hills overlooking the ocean, they spot a vehicle plunge off a cliff.

Speeding down the trail to rescue the driver, they are nearly run down by the suspect car, which quickly disappears. As Tilly pursues justice for the victim, she is confronted by a paranoid perpetrator, ancient vendettas, and chilling discoveries.

Can Tilly navigate the wild maneuvers of the menacing motorist or will she be the next victim of the rogue racer?

ABOUT THE AUTHOR

Sue Hollowell is a wife and empty nester with a lot of mom left over. Finding a lot of time on her hands, and as a lover of mystery novels, she began telling the story of a character who appeared in her head.

The Chemical Bond is a book about Meredith Markette, a young woman who reluctantly enters into the field of law enforcement when her police officer father is killed in the line of duty. Her quest is to discover his murderer and in the meantime come to terms with a tragedy of her youth.

Will this book ever see the light of day? Maybe. Sue really likes the story and character. And writing that book taught her a ton about the publishing industry. Through this experience she has discovered a love of writing stories, and especially mysteries. She hopes you enjoy her books as much as she enjoys writing them.

Connect with Sue on Facebook at www.facebook.com/sueh ollowellauthor and sign up for her newsletter to stay in touch with all things cozy!